Ten Apples Up On Top!

by Theo. LeSieg

Illustrated by
Roy McKie

BEGINNER BOOKS

A Division of Random House, Inc.

This title was originally catalogued by the Library of Congress as follows: Seuss, Dr. Ten apples up on top! By Theo. LeSieg [pseud.] Illustrated by Roy McKie. [New York] Beginner Books [1961] 59 p. illus. 24 cm. I. Title. PZ8.3.G276Te 61-7068 rev ISBN 0-394-80019-2 ISBN 0-394-90019-7 (lib. bdg.)

 Published in New York by Random House, Inc., and simultaneously in Toronto, Canada, by Random House of Canada, Limited. Manufactured in the United States of America.

One apple
up on top!

Two apples
up on top!

Look, you.

I can do it, too.

Look!

See!

I can do three!

Three . . .

Three . . .

I see.

I see.

You can do three
but I can do more.
You have three
but I have four.

Look! See, now.
I can hop
with four apples
up on top.

And I can hop
up on a tree
with four apples
up on me.

Look here, you two.

See here, you two.

I can get five

on top.

Can you?

I am so good
I will not stop.
Five!
Now six!
Now seven on top!

Seven apples
up on top!

I am
so good
they will not drop.

Five, six, seven!
Fun, fun, fun!
Seven, six, five,
four, three, two, one!

But, see!
We are as good as you.
Look! Now we
have seven, too.

And now, see here.
Eight! Eight on top!
Eight apples up!
Not one will drop.

Eight! Eight!
And we can skate.
Look now!
We can skate
with eight.

But I can do nine.
And hop!
And drink!
You can not do this,
I think.

We can! We can!

We can do it, too.

See here.

We are as good as you!

We all are very good
I think.
With nine, we all
can hop and drink.

Nine is very good.
But then . . .
Come on and we
will make it ten!

Look!

Ten

apples

up

on

top!

We are not

going to let them drop!

Look out!
Look out!
I see a mop.

I will make
the apples fall.
Get out. Get out. You!
One and all!

Come on! Come on!
Come down this hall.
We must not let
our apples fall!

Out of our way!
We can not stop.
We can not let
our apples drop.

This is not good.
What will we do?
They want to get
our apples, too.

They will get them
if we let them.
Come! We can not
let them get them.

Look out!

The mop!

The mop!

The mop!

You can not stop
our apple fun.
Our apples will not drop.
Not one!

Come on! Come on!
Come one! Come all!
We have to make
the apples fall.

They must not get
our apples down.
Come on! Come on!
Get out of town!

Apples!

Apples up on top!

All of this

must stop

STOP

STOP!

Now all our fun
is going to stop!
Our apples all
are going to drop.

Look!
Ten apples
on us all!

What fun!
We will not
let them fall.